The Boxcar Children Mysteries

The Boxcar Children Mysteries

THE MYSTERY OF THE STOLEN DINOSAUR BONES

created by
GERTRUDE CHANDLER WARNER

WITHDRAWN

Albert Whitman & Company
Chicago, Illinois

Library of Congress Cataloging-in-Publication data
is on file with the publisher.

Copyright © 2015 by Albert Whitman & Company
Published in 2015 by Albert Whitman & Company
978-0-8075-5608-5 (hardcover)
978-0-8075-5609-2 (paperback)

THE BOXCAR CHILDREN® is a registered
trademark of Albert Whitman & Company.

Printed in the United States of America
10 9 8 7 6 5 4 3 2 1 LB 20 19 18 17 16 15 14

Cover art by Logan Kline
Interior illustrations by Anthony VanArsdale

For more information about Albert Whitman & Company,
visit our web site at www.albertwhitman.com.

Contents

CHAPTER 1

Stolen Bones

"Look at the huge, blue sky!" said Violet Alden. She snapped photos through the window of the shuttle van. Violet was ten, and she loved to paint and photograph beautiful things.

Her twelve-year-old sister, Jessie, sat next to her. She looked out the window over Violet's shoulder.

"I've never seen so much blue sky either. It seems to go on forever," she said.

"That's why people call Montana 'Big Sky Country,'" said Henry. Violet and Jessie's older brother sat behind his sisters. He was reading from a brochure he had picked up at the airport. Henry was fourteen and liked to learn all he could about things. "It looks like we're getting close to the Hell Creek Formation. Paleontologists from around the world come to study the fossils that are found there."

"Elliot's ranch must be close too," said Jessie. "It will be fun to join him on his dinosaur dig!"

The Aldens were going to visit Elliot Boyce, a paleontologist who was a friend of their grandfather's.

"Hell Creek Formation was once home to thousands of dinosaurs," said Henry. "And their bones have been found all throughout this area. Including T. rex bones!"

"I hope we find a T. rex," said Benny. "Or maybe we'll find a dinosaur that nobody has ever seen before!" Benny was six-years-old, the youngest of the Alden children. He was always excited about new adventures.

James Alden looked back at his four grandchildren from the front passenger's seat. "I wouldn't be surprised if you had a dinosaur named after you, Benny," he said. "You children never fail to amaze me!"

The four Alden children smiled at their grandfather. When their parents died, they had run away and lived in a boxcar in the woods. They knew that they had a grandfather, but they had heard that he was mean. When Grandfather finally found them, they learned that he was a very nice man. They went to live with him along with Watch, the dog they had rescued while they lived in the boxcar. Grandfather had a big house in Greenfield, Connecticut. He also had a big backyard and moved the boxcar there for the children to play in.

Watch leaped onto Henry's lap and started barking at something outside the window. Henry laughed as he rescued his brochure. "What do you see, Watch?" he asked.

"It's a herd of bison!" exclaimed Violet. She took photos of the grazing animals.

"There are all kinds of wildlife that live in Montana," said Henry. "In fact, Montana might have more animals than people!"

"And some of those animals were huge!" said Benny. "Like an apatosaurus!"

"You're right about that, Benny, "said Jessie. "It's fun to think about dinosaurs out there grazing, just like that herd of bison."

The driver pulled the van into the parking lot of a large wooden building with a big sign.

"*Hogan's Museum and Diner,*" said Benny, carefully pronouncing each word. Benny was just learning how to read big words. He loved to practice by reading signs.

"This is where we're supposed to meet Elliot," said Jessie.

The Aldens unloaded their bags and waved good-bye to the shuttle driver.

Just then a young man with curly red hair and a scraggly beard approached them. He smiled when he saw Grandfather Alden and held out his hand. "James! My goodness, it has been a long time!"

He and Grandfather shook hands. "Yes, it has, Elliot," said Grandfather. "I haven't seen you since you graduated from college."

Violet shyly studied Elliot. He was wearing muddy work clothes, which Violet thought was an odd way to dress in public.

"You've never met my grandchildren," said Grandfather. He introduced Henry, Jessie, Violet, and Benny to Elliot, and Elliot shook each by the hand.

"It's very nice to meet you," said Elliot.

"Same here!" said Benny. "When will we start digging dinosaur bones?"

"Let's go in the diner for some lunch first," said Elliot, laughing. "Then we can visit my dig. It'll be fun to show you my exciting find, but we should eat first!"

"Lunch is a great idea!" said Benny. "I like to dig for dinosaurs, but I also like to eat!"

"Thank you, Elliot," said Jessie, laughing. "Lunch sounds like a good idea."

The Aldens put their bags into Elliot's jeep. Watch jumped into the jeep and wagged his tail. They gave him some water then headed into the diner, which was right next to the museum. They sat down at a table and looked around. The walls were covered with mounted dinosaur skulls.

"This place is sort of scary," said Violet. "All those skulls look as if they're alive!"

Jessie smiled. She was always motherly toward her younger siblings. "Those dinosaurs have been dead for a long time, Violet. They can't hurt you."

"Hello." A woman wearing a colorful apron over a T-shirt and jeans appeared at their table. She had a pad and pen in her hands. "What can I get you?" she asked. "We have a soup and sandwich special this weekend."

"That sounds perfect," said Mr. Alden. Everyone agreed. The woman took their order and quickly walked away. Jessie noticed that she had scowled at Elliot before turning away.

The woman soon returned with a tray of soup and sandwiches.

"I like your apron!" said Benny. "That's a triceratops, right?"

"It's a Torosaurus," said the woman. She wasn't smiling.

"I haven't seen you before," said Elliot.

"Mickey is on a break," said the woman. "I'm the owner. I'm usually in back. Do you folks need anything else?"

"I think this will do," said Mr. Alden. "Thank you."

The woman hurried away.

"It seemed as if she didn't want to talk to us," said Jessie.

"She looks sort of familiar," said Elliot. "But I don't know where I've seen her before."

After lunch the children decided to look around the museum while Grandfather and Elliot had coffee and visited. The museum walls were covered with fossils, tools, framed photographs, and clippings from newspapers and magazines. The children got closer to study the photographs. The woman who had served their lunch joined them.

"That's my great-grandfather," she said. She pointed to one of the photos on the wall. "His name was Bones Hogan. This was his museum a long time ago."

"And now you own it," said Jessie. She wondered why the woman was being friendly to them now.

"That's right," said the woman. "My name is Jolanda Hogan."

"It's nice to meet you," said Jessie. "My family is here visiting. We want to dig for dinosaur bones!"

"You kids have come to the right place," said Jolanda. "You may even find a real dinosaur while you're here! My great-grandfather used to say that dinosaurs are still among us." Jolanda laughed. "Of course we all know that dinosaurs are extinct," she said.

"Wow, look at the scary skull in this photo," said Violet. She pointed to a photograph of a large, bearded man pointing at fossil remains next to him.

"That T. rex was one of my grandfather's best finds," said Jolanda. "Bones Hogan sold that dinosaur to a big museum in Washington, DC.

"I bet he got a lot of money for it!" said Benny.

Elliot had explained over lunch that collectors and museums bought dinosaur bones. The rarer the bones, the more valuable they were.

"Oh, money wasn't important to Bones," said Jolanda. "Though he needed money to run this museum." She sighed. "Bones is long gone now anyway."

"Look, there are Grandfather and Elliot. It

must be time to go," said Jessie. "We'll come back soon!"

Jolanda looked over at Elliot standing by the doorway. Violet noticed that she was scowling. Jolanda turned and smiled at the Aldens. "Please come visit my museum anytime," she said.

In the parking lot, a tall man with dark, slicked-back hair greeted Elliot. They shook hands and Elliot introduced the Aldens to Warren Gordon.

"Mr. Gordon buys fossils for a museum back east," said Elliot.

"Nice to meet you all," said Mr. Gordon. "Elliot, we'll talk later about that find you told me about!"

"Yes, we will," said Elliot, smiling.

Mr. Gordon waved as he headed into Hogan's Museum.

***

The Aldens piled into Elliot's jeep and headed down the bumpy and dusty road. Watch barked when a roadrunner raced by.

"Did you know that birds are descendants of dinosaurs?" asked Elliot.

"There are a lot of theories about that," said Henry.

"That's true, Henry," said Elliot. "We learn new things about dinosaurs almost every day!"

"Birds today are much smaller than most dinosaurs," said Benny. "That's a fact."

"That's okay with me!" said Violet.

Everyone laughed as Elliot pulled onto a side road.

"Let's stop at my dig and I'll show you my latest find," said Elliot. "I'm so excited about it. From what I've read, nothing like it has ever been found before!"

He pulled the jeep over and everyone got out. Elliot led them to a spot in the brush. There was a big hole that was almost hidden from view.

"It's a cave!" said Benny. "We love caves."

"Well, then, follow me!" said Elliot. He pulled a flashlight from his pocket.

"Watch and I will stand guard," said Grandfather. He smiled as the children crawled after Elliot through the hole. The hole led to a passageway.

Elliot shined his flashlight to light their way. Henry, Jessie, Violet, and Benny followed. The passage soon opened up into a tall cavern. The children could hear water dripping somewhere in the dark. The air was much cooler than outside. Elliot leaned down and flipped on a lantern sitting on the cave floor. The cave suddenly lit up in the soft glow.

"This reminds me of Dragon's Mouth Cavern," said Violet.

"Yes, it does!" said Jessie. "Remember when we…"

Suddenly Elliot gasped. "Oh no! Oh no!" he exclaimed. "Somebody stole my dinosaur bones!"

CHAPTER 2

Caving Adventure

Elliot shined his flashlight around the edges of the cave. "The dinosaur bones that I stored here are all gone! They've been stolen!"

"How awful!" said Jessie.

"Were there a lot of bones?" asked Henry.

"It was just a small collection of leg bone fragments, but they were part of my big find," said Elliot. "I had them stored in a cloth sack." He slumped against a wall and shook his head. "If I don't have all the bones, I won't get to say I found it all by myself."

He looked around the cave again and sighed. "I'm going to look outside. He headed toward the passageway.

"We'll be right there," said Henry.

Suddenly the Aldens were alone in the cave.

"It's spooky in here," said Violet. "Look at the scary shadows on the walls!"

"It's just the light from the lantern playing tricks," said Jessie. She put her arm around her sister.

"I've heard of bank robbers, but who would take dinosaur bones?" asked Benny.

"That's a good question," said Henry. He picked up the lantern and shined it around the cave, making the shadows move.

Violet tried not to look at the creepy shadows. She noticed two square-shaped marks in the floor in front of a wall. "Look at those marks," she said, pointing.

Henry shined the lantern close to the marks. "I wonder what made those." He shined the lantern up the wall. "Hey," he said, "there's a big hole up there!"

"Oh," said Jessie. "We'll need a ladder to get that high."

"Maybe that's what these square marks are," said Violet. "A ladder was placed here."

"You have good eyes, Violet," said Jessie. "You've already solved the mystery!"

"Well, not exactly," said Violet. "We haven't found the missing bones yet."

"Or the thief," Benny pointed out.

"But we're on the right track," said Henry. "It looks like the thief came down here, took the bones, and went back up, using a ladder."

"We need to tell Elliot!" said Jessie. "Let's go!"

The children climbed out of the cave and joined Elliot and Grandfather, who were talking.

"I found that cave a few days ago," Elliot was saying. "I thought it would be a perfect place to stash my finds." Elliot sighed. "I guess I was wrong!"

"It appears that someone else knew about this cave," said Grandfather.

"There aren't any other tire tracks though," said Elliot. "There are only the ones from my jeep." He scratched his head.

Grandfather noticed Benny shifting from one foot to the other. "Oh, it looks as if my grandchildren have something to tell us," he said. "Did you find something?"

"Yes," said Jessie. "We think we know what happened!"

The children took turns telling Elliot and Grandfather about their discovery. Perhaps the thief had come down a ladder, stolen the bones, and gone back the same way! The cave must have another entrance.

"It's funny that I didn't notice another passageway before," said Elliot. He chuckled. "I guess I'm always looking down, looking for bones!" Then Elliot became serious again. "I need to make some phone calls right away," he said. "We need to go to the house."

"Maybe we can come back and look for the other entrance to the cave," said Henry.

"Yes, that's a good idea," said Elliot. "Let's get going."

"Where is Watch?" asked Violet.

"Oh, look, he's over there digging," said Benny. He ran over to Watch and bent over to see what their dog was digging up. "Oh!

Watch found a fossil!" he cried. "Is it one of the stolen bones?"

"No," said Elliot. "But it is a toe bone from the same dinosaur!" He pulled a small roll of tape and a marker from his pocket. "It's the fifty-fourth bone found so far." Elliot wrote *54 E.B.* on a piece of tape. He secured it to the toe bone as Benny held it up.

"This is your toe bone," said Benny. "Watch found it for you." He handed the bone to Elliot.

"Thank you, Benny," said Elliot.

"And we'll try to find the stolen bones!" said Violet.

"That would be great," said Elliot. He put the toe bone in his pocket. "Now let's get going."

At the ranch, the Aldens unpacked. They put their things away while Grandfather and Elliot made phone calls. Since the dinosaur Elliot had found was very rare, Elliot explained that the thief could be trying to sell it quickly before he got caught. Elliot called on the people that he knew in the business. Once the word was out that the bones were stolen, it would be hard for the thief to sell them.

"I hope you can find clues about who stole my dinosaur bones," said Elliot. He showed the Aldens where he kept equipment for caving. The children put small packs together. Jessie and Henry helped Bennie and Violet strap on caving helmets. Then Henry grabbed a folding ladder. "I think we're ready to explore!" he said. The children and Watch headed back to the dig site.

***

Watch followed the children into the cave. "Do you smell any clues, Watch?" Jessie asked. Watch sniffed around the floor. He stopped near the ladder marks and looked up and wagged his tail.

"I think Watch wants us to go up into that passageway too," said Violet.

"He sniffs something," said Jessie.

"Let's check it out," said Henry. "I'll go first."

Henry and Jessie set their ladder against the cave wall. Henry climbed up while Jessie held the ladder steady. He shined his headlight into the passageway before crawling in.

"Be careful," called Violet. She looked around nervously. The shadows from their flashlights made the cave walls look like they were alive.

"I think I hear something," whispered Benny. He shined his flashlight on a dark corner. Something scurried out of the light beam.

"What is it?" cried Violet.

Jessie slowly walked over and shined her light around the cave floor. She gasped as a dark brown mouse scampered between her feet and zipped across the floor. It disappeared inside a crack in the wall.

"What else lives inside this cave?" asked Violet. She shivered.

"Henry," Jessie called. "Watch out for cave creatures up there!"

Just then Henry poked his head out of the passageway. "Come on up!" he said. "Just watch your step."

Jessie helped Benny and Violet up. Then Jessie handed up Watch and crawled in after him. There was room for everyone to crouch. The passageway headed into the darkness.

"We just have to crawl for a few feet, then the passageway gets taller and wider," said Henry. "It's very dark and some places are muddy."

"We'll be very careful," said Jessie. "And stick together. Right, everyone?"

The children agreed. They crawled slowly through the rocky passageway. The bright lights on their caving helmets and their flashlights showed the way. Soon the passageway became large enough for the children to stand up.

"Look over there," said Violet. She pointed to an opening. The children saw a small cavern just below them. "Should we go in there?"

"I think so," said Jessie. "We'll all go together and keep close."

They carefully stepped into the cavern and shined their flashlights around the floor.

"Oh, I see some tracks," said Violet. "They're in the mud by that opening in the wall."

Jessie tiptoed over and shined her light on the cave floor. She drew in her breath and looked back at her siblings.

"What's wrong?" asked Henry. "Are

they footprints?" They joined Jessie by the muddy tracks.

"Oh, those aren't footprints," said Violet.

"Not from a person," said Jessie. "They look like bird tracks..."

"Very big bird tracks!" said Violet. "They're huge! What kind of bird makes tracks that big?" She looked around and hugged herself.

"I know!" cried Benny. "It's a real, live dinosaur!"

Just then Watch started barking.

CHAPTER 3

A Cave Full of Bones

The children stood still and listened. Watch stopped barking.

"Were those footsteps?" asked Violet. "I thought I heard footsteps."

"It must be the dinosaur!" said Benny.

"There are no dinosaurs living today," said Henry.

The children waited. The sound of footsteps stopped.

"Whatever it is got too far away for us to hear," said Jessie.

"Or it stopped," said Violet. She held tight to her sister's hand.

"Watch doesn't look worried," said Jessie. "It's too bad he can't talk!" She petted Watch as he wagged his tail.

"I'm sure there's an explanation for these tracks," said Henry. He bent to study them again.

"Maybe they were made from treads on someone's shoes. Some shoes leave strange patterns," said Jessie.

"I just hope whatever made the tracks has left," said Violet.

"I think whoever or whatever made the tracks is gone now," said Henry. "Or else Watch would tell us. So let's keep exploring."

The children headed back into the passageway. Violet posted a sticky note on the entry to the little cavern and wrote *strange tracks* with a shaky hand.

"That's a good idea to mark our way," said Jessie. "We don't want to get lost in here!"

"I'm also drawing a map of the cave in my sketchbook," said Violet. "It keeps me from getting too scared!"

The children walked along slowly. They were careful to check all around as they made their way down the passage. They barely squeezed through a small tunnel that led to another wide passage.

"I don't think anyone much bigger than us could get through there," said Jessie. "That was a tight fit!"

"Caves can have hundreds of miles of passages of all sizes," said Henry. "Many caves have never been explored before or even discovered."

"It looks as if this one has been discovered," said Violet. She pointed to a plastic bag lying in the passageway. The children examined the little bag.

"There's something inside," said Benny. "It looks sort of like popcorn before it's been popped!"

Henry picked up the bag and shined his light on the contents. "It's dried corn!" he said. "It's a very odd thing to find inside a cave!"

"Let's take it with us," suggested Violet. "Maybe it's a clue about who took Elliot's dinosaur bones." She put the bag inside her pack.

"Look ahead of us," said Benny. "I see light! Did we walk in a circle?"

Henry checked his compass. "No, we've been walking east since we started. That light must be another entry to the cave!"

"Or maybe the dinosaur has his lights on," said Benny. His brother and sisters laughed, though Violet looked around nervously. They continued along the passage. Soon they entered a huge cavern with a large entry opposite where they stood. Sunlight streamed inside. The Aldens turned off their helmet lights and looked around.

"It looks like we found the other entrance," said Jessie.

"And it looks like someone uses this side of the cave," said Henry.

The children were surrounded by boxes and blue plastic crates. There were bones in piles all over the floor. The boxes and crates were overflowing with more bones and rocks.

"It looks like a paleontologist uses this cave," said Jessie. "I wonder who."

"Jolanda said that Bones Hogan was 'long

gone.' Does that mean he disappeared?" asked Violet.

"I thought Jolanda meant that he died but maybe not," said Henry. He rubbed his chin as he looked around. "Look, those are fresh boot prints in the mud," he said. "It's like someone was just here. We should be careful and talk softly."

"Do you think Elliot's stolen dinosaur bones are here?" whispered Benny.

"I don't know," said Henry. "We'll have to look for them."

"Elliot's bones will be marked," said Benny. "A piece of tape will have a number and his initials." He smiled.

"Good work, Benny," said Jessie. "You know because that's how Elliot marked the toe bone that you found."

Benny beamed with pride.

"I'll take photos of everything," whispered Violet. She walked around the cavern, snapping photos with her camera. The other children studied the piles of bones. They carefully sifted through the boxes and crates.

"I don't see any bones that are marked *E.B.*," said Benny.

"I don't either," said Jessie.

Henry nodded agreement.

"We should also check those," said Jessie, pointing to three openings in the cavern's walls. The children could see even more caverns through each opening.

"You're right, Jessie," said Henry. "Let's stick together. We want to be ready in case whoever uses this cave shows up."

"Whoever—or *whatever*—uses this cave, you mean," said Benny.

The children headed into the first cavern. Inside were metal crates filled with tools. "These look like digging and cleaning tools," said Henry. "There are chisels, hammers, picks, and all kinds of brushes."

"There are lots of shovels in this crate," said Jessie.

"These are the tools that dinosaur hunters use to dig up bones," said Benny.

Violet was studying a small chisel. "This chisel has letters carved in the wooden handle," she said. She held it up for everyone to see.

"*B.H.*," said Benny.

"Those are probably the owner's initials," said Henry. "People working together on a dig might mark their tools so that they don't confuse them." He looked around the cavern again. "I don't see any bones in this cavern."

The children carefully made their way to the second cavern. There were stacks of books and piles of papers but no bones. They headed to the third cavern. It was very small. There was a wooden table and a chair. A kerosene lamp sat on the table next to an open book. A sleeping bag lay nearby. It looked as if someone had used it recently.

Henry carefully picked up the book. "*Dinosaur Birds by Bones Hogan*," he read. "This is a book about giant dinosaur birds!"

"The *B.H.* on the pick must stand for Bones Hogan," said Benny. "He lives here! And he has a dinosaur bird that lives with him!"

"Please stop saying that, Benny," said Violet. "You know dinosaurs are extinct!" She looked nervous again.

"I'm sorry, Violet," said Benny. "I know you don't want to see a live dinosaur. But I do!"

"This mystery is getting more and more interesting," said Henry. "Let's go outside and see what else we can find."

The children passed through the wide opening. They stood in a narrow, rocky valley.

Craggy hills and scrubby trees surrounded the valley.

"It looks like a faraway planet," said Benny.

"Where someone lives," said Henry. "And whoever lives here would probably not like finding us here."

"Especially if it's the dinosaur bone thief," said Violet.

The children headed back into the cave. Watch ran ahead and began to bark again. They quickly caught up with him in the cavern with the piles of papers. He was sniffing at another opening on another side of the cavern.

"Oh! We didn't notice that before," said Henry.

"I think we'd better leave—now," said Jessie.

"I think so too!" said Violet.

"Let's see what's through that hole," said Benny. "Please? Then we can leave."

"Okay," said Henry. "I'm curious too!" The children agreed and headed through the opening and into a dark cavern. They turned their helmet lights back on.

"I don't see anything," said Jessie. They walked around, shining their lights on the floor and walls. "Oh wait. Look at this!" Jessie picked something up from the floor. She held it up to her helmet light.

"That's a feather," said Violet.

"It's a very big feather!" said Benny. He grinned in the darkness.

Henry shined his flashlight around the floor. He pointed at white spots on the rocks. "It looks like a bird uses this cavern. Maybe whoever lives here has a parrot."

"A parrot doesn't have giant feet," Benny pointed out.

"Or giant feathers," said Violet.

Just then a voice bellowed from behind the children. "What do you kids think you're doing in here?"

CHAPTER 4

Dinosaur Dan

A very tall man with a long, scraggly gray beard glared at the Aldens.

Benny noticed that the man looked like one of the photos back at the museum. "Are you Bones Hogan?" he asked shyly.

"Heck no, I'm not Bones Hogan, young man," bellowed the man. "Just how old do you think I am? And who are you people?" He scowled at the children.

The children quickly introduced themselves.

"You also look a little like Santa Claus," said Benny.

"Well, I ain't him either," chuckled the man. "People call me Dinosaur Dan."

Watch ran over to Dinosaur Dan and sniffed at his boots.

"And who is this little rascal?" asked Dinosaur Dan. He let Watch smell his hand. Then he tickled Watch under his chin.

"That's our dog, Watch," said Jessie.

"It's a pleasure to meet you, Watch," said Dinosaur Dan. "I used to have a dog that looked just like you, only bigger." He chuckled and petted Watch on the head.

"Do you have a pet dinosaur now?" asked Benny.

Dinosaur Dan burst out laughing. His laugh echoed around the cavern. Benny decided that Dinosaur Dan also sounded like Santa Claus. "What a question! Why do you ask?" he asked.

"Um, because we saw what looked like giant bird tracks and a giant feather inside the cave," said Violet.

"That is very *interesting*," said Dinosaur Dan with just the slightest smile. "You know that dinosaurs like coelurosaurs had birdlike feet and feathers, right?"

"I know about coelurosaurs!" said Benny.

"But dinosaurs are extinct!" said Jessie.

"Sure, that's what they say," said Dinosaur Dan. "But what do they know? I'd watch your step in that cave, that's all I can say."

"We will," said Violet. She clutched Jessie's hand again.

Jessie looked at Dinosaur Dan. Something about the way he was smiling made her wonder if he knew more about the tracks than he let on.

"So why don't you tell me what you kids are doing in my cave?" asked Dinosaur Dan.

"We're very sorry if we trespassed," said Henry. "We didn't know that someone owned this side of the cave."

"I don't know what you mean by that," said Dinosaur Dan. "There's another side?"

"Yes, our friend has a dinosaur dig on the other side of this cave," explained Henry. "He stored some bones there."

"And somebody stole them!" blurted Benny.

"Huh," said Dinosaur Dan. "Well, I'm a lot of things, but I ain't no thief. Who is your friend anyway?"

"Our friend's name is Elliot Boyce," said Jessie. "He is a paleontologist."

The children noticed that Dinosaur Dan frowned when Jessie said Elliot's name.

"Elliot Boyce, eh?" said Dinosaur Dan.

"We think somebody took his dinosaur bones and came this way," said Henry. "That's how we ended up here."

"We didn't know someone lived here," added Violet.

"Well, I sure live here," said Dinosaur Dan. "I lease the property and hunt for dinosaur bones. I guess you saw my collection since you were nosing around in my stuff."

"Yes, you have a lot of dinosaur bones," said Benny.

"I do indeed," said Dinosaur Dan. "And I can tell you like dinosaurs, Benny," he said, grinning.

Benny grinned back at the big man.

"As for Elliot Boyce, he's nothing but a thief himself," said Dinosaur Dan. "I'm glad somebody stole something from him!"

Violet frowned. She didn't like to hear that a friend of Grandfather's might be a thief. She looked at Henry.

"Why would you say that about Elliot?" asked Henry. "He's a good friend of our Grandfather's."

"Maybe Elliot has pulled the wool over your grandfather's eyes," said Dinosaur Dan. "But he was a thief."

"When was Elliot a thief?" asked Violet.

"It happened when were in college," said Dinosaur Dan.

Benny looked at Dinosaur Dan's gray beard and looked puzzled.

Dinosaur Dan smiled at Benny. "I was a little old for college, but so what? I wanted to be a paleontologist."

"What happened?" Jessie asked politely.

"Elliot and I were very good friends," said Dinosaur Dan. "We discovered some dinosaur bones out in Hell Creek. It was a very important find."

"What kind of dinosaur was it?" asked Benny.

"It was a coelurosaur," said Dinosaur Dan. "It was a kind that nobody had ever discovered before."

"What happened?" asked Henry.

"My so-called friend Elliot stole our findings. He took my name off everything and got all the credit." Dinosaur Dan pulled off his leather hat and slapped it on his knee. The hat sent a billow of dust into the air. "I was so mad I walked out of college and never looked back," he said. "I moved out here. Now I just do what I do best, hunt for bones."

The Aldens looked at one another. "We're so sorry to hear that Elliot may have cheated you," said Jessie. "Maybe it was a misunderstanding."

"Maybe you can talk to him," said Violet, "since he lives nearby."

"He probably has a good explanation," said Henry.

Benny nodded.

"I don't care where he lives. I got no interest in talking to that thief," said Dinosaur Dan. "Like I said, I'm done with all that. Come on, I'll show you how I spend my time these days."

The children followed Dinosaur Dan. They listened as he talked about his finds. He said that his little valley had never been explored before.

"I've found lots of common dinosaurs here," said Dinosaur Dan. "I've found some rare ones too."

"What do you do with the bones you find?" asked Jessie.

"I sell some to collectors and museums," said Dinosaur Dan. "Others I donate to schools. It depends."

"How do you keep people from finding out where you are?" asked Violet.

"I have a secret way out of this valley," said Dinosaur Dan. "I have a camp about a mile away. It looks like I live there." He chuckled. "But I don't."

"You live in the cave!" said Benny.

"That's right, Benny!" said Dinosaur Dan.

"You didn't know the cave had another entrance?" asked Henry.

Dinosaur Dan glared at Henry. Violet noticed that Dinosaur Dan's moods seemed to change very quickly.

"What I know or don't know ain't none of your business," said Dinosaur Dan. "You kids should probably leave now. I have to arrange a meeting with that Warren Gordon fellow for tomorrow. Then I have to pick up supplies." He pulled out a cell phone and waved for the children to go away.

"Thank you for showing us around!" said Henry. Dinosaur Dan grunted. Henry motioned for his brother and sisters to join him. They turned and headed back to the cave entrance.

"What is that?" asked Benny. The children saw a shadow duck quickly inside the cave. Watch ran ahead, barking.

"Was that a person?" asked Violet.

"Maybe it was the dinosaur," said Benny. "Now I'm not so sure that I want to meet it." He huddled close to Henry.

"Let's just be careful," said Henry, taking Benny's hand. The children slowly entered the big cavern and looked around. Watch stopped barking.

"Whatever or whoever it was is gone," said Jessie.

"Let's go back to the ranch," said Violet. "I don't think I want to meet a real dinosaur either."

"Good idea, Violet," said Jessie. "I think we've worn out our welcome here."

The children turned their helmet lights on and started back through the passageway. Soon they passed the opening to the cavern where they had found the strange tracks.

"Yikes, what was that?" asked Violet.

Scratching noises were coming from inside the dark cavern. Watch yipped and stared at the opening, wagging his tail.

"Something or someone is in there," whispered Henry. "Right now."

"I think we should just keep going," whispered Jessie. She snatched Watch up into her arms and grabbed Violet's hand. "Let's get out of here."

The children raced back through the passageway as the scratching sounds faded in the distance.

CHAPTER 5

A Different Story

Henry climbed down the ladder first. Jessie handed Watch to Henry and then she and the others climbed down one after the other. The children brushed their dusty clothes with their hands. They stomped their feet and scraped mud off of their shoes.

"That was scary!" said Benny. He wiped his hands on a towel that Jessie gave him.

"What was making that scratching sound?" asked Violet.

"I don't know," said Jessie. "We also saw

that shadow at the cave entrance."

"That could have been a person," said Henry. "Or maybe it was a big dog."

"Dinosaur Dan said he used to have a dog. He doesn't have one now," said Benny. "Maybe it really is a dinosaur."

"I'm just glad whatever it was stayed inside the cave!" said Violet.

"Me too," said Jessie. "Let's go back to the ranch."

"Good idea," said Henry. "It's getting very late."

Henry folded up the ladder and stashed it in the cave, and the children started for the ranch.

"Dinosaur Dan told us a lot of stories," said Jessie.

"I wonder why he said that Elliot stole his college project," said Violet. "We should ask Elliot about that."

"We will," said Henry.

The children arrived at the ranch. Grandfather was sitting on the deck, reading. He put his book down and smiled. "Did you find the missing dinosaur bones?" he asked.

Henry, Jessie, Violet, and Benny surrounded Grandfather. They all started talking at once.

"Hold on, what? A man lives on the other side of the cave?" he asked.

"That's right," said Jessie. "And he said that a real dinosaur might be in the cave!"

"That would be very interesting," chuckled Grandfather. "I'm glad you had Watch with you," he added.

"Yes, Watch protected us," said Violet.

"We'd like to go back tomorrow to look some more," said Henry.

"That's okay with me," said Grandfather. "Elliot appreciates your help very much."

"Where is Elliot?" asked Jessie. "We want to talk to him."

"He's out in his shop," said Grandfather. "Why don't you go tell him about your discovery and I'll heat up some chili for dinner."

"What a good idea!" said Benny.

"Oh, Benny, you know that we always make sure that you eat," said Jessie.

The children headed to the shop. The

large building was in the backyard. It was surrounded by heaps of gravel and dirt.

They found Elliot working at a table inside. Elliot's shop was crowded with tables, tools, and boxes of bones that were embedded in dirt and rock. The walls were lined with more tables that displayed bones of all kinds and sizes. The old wooden floor was nearly covered with more boxes.

"Look at all the dinosaur bones," said Benny. "It's like a museum in here!"

Elliot turned. "Hey, it's good to see you guys," he said. "Did you find my missing dinosaur bones?" he asked.

"We didn't find the bones," said Henry.

"But we are going back tomorrow," said Jessie.

"I called everyone I could think of," said Elliot. "Hopefully if the thief tries to sell the bones, he will be caught." He sighed. "But without those bones my rare find will never be complete."

"How do you put together a dinosaur?" asked Henry.

Jessie smiled at her brother. She knew he

wanted to get Elliot to think about something else.

"Well, as you can see, I have endless piles of rocks and dirt," Elliot explained. "It's the stuff that I chip away from the treasures."

"You mean the dinosaur bones," said Benny.

"Yes, dinosaur bones are the treasures, Benny," said Elliot. He smiled.

"Restoring dinosaur bones can be more difficult than finding them," continued Elliot. "It can take months, even years, to clean and assemble a dinosaur."

"Wow, you have a lot of tools!" said Henry.

"That tool is called an air scribe," said Elliot, pointing at the tool that Henry was admiring. "We call it a micro-jackhammer." He held up another air tool. "This is a tiny sandblaster. They all work using compressed air. I also use dental tools to do fine cleaning."

"You're a dinosaur dentist!" said Benny.

Everyone laughed.

"The early dinosaur bone hunters would have appreciated these tools," said Henry. "All they had were picks and hammers."

"That's true," said Elliot. "And sometimes, valuable bones were destroyed when they were excavated. Now we use tools that are very gentle and precise."

"The bones can be very fragile," said Henry. "They might be softer than the rock around them."

"That's exactly right, Henry," said Elliot. He showed the children some cleaned bones from his recent find.

"That looks like a skull," said Benny.

"It is a skull," said Elliot. "It's part of the dinosaur that I found by the cave. I think it's a dinosaur related to one I found back when I was in college."

Jessie looked at Henry.

"What did you find while you were in college?" Henry asked.

"It was a rare kind of coelurosaur," said Elliot. "My good friend Dan and I discovered it. We were working together on a school project." Suddenly Elliot frowned.

"Did something happen with your school project?" Jessie asked.

"Oh, something happened all right," said

Elliot. "My so-called friend jumped ship."

"There was a ship?" Benny asked.

"I think Elliot means that his friend left," explained Violet.

"Yes, my friend Dan left," said Elliot. "And he took all his notes with him. I had to present the project by myself." Elliot picked up a pile of dirt from a table. He flung it to the floor. "That guy almost cost me my college degree."

"That's awful," said Violet. She felt bad for Elliot. He looked very angry.

"But you got your degree," said Jessie. "Grandfather was there for your graduation!"

"That's true," said Elliot. He smiled again. "Now I'm doing what I love to do."

"Do you think maybe it was a misunderstanding?" asked Violet. "Between you and your friend Dan?"

Elliot scowled again. "None of that matters anymore," he said. "Let's check out that toe bone that Benny found this morning. I've been working on it."

The children followed Elliot to a workspace on another table to admire the toe bone. "This morning it looked like a rock with something

sticking out of it," said Benny. "Now it looks just like a toe bone!"

"That's how it goes when we hunt for dinosaur bones," said Elliot. "It's always a treasure hunt."

***

"We still need to tell Elliot that we found Dan," said Jessie.

The children were gathered in the guest room getting ready for bed. Grandfather and Elliot were watching an old movie in the living room.

"But we don't know if Dan is the one who stole the bones," said Henry. "Maybe we should wait to tell Elliot about him."

"You're right," said Jessie. "We'll look more carefully tomorrow. Maybe we'll find the bones in Dan's collection."

"I just thought of something!" said Benny.

"What's that?" asked Jessie. She knew that Benny sometimes noticed things that the rest of them missed.

"Dan said that he was going to meet someone tomorrow," said Benny.

"That's a good thing to remember!" said Henry.

"He said that he's going to meet Mr. Gordon, the buyer," said Violet. "Maybe he's going to sell him the stolen bones."

"We better get up early then," said Jessie. "We need to find the bones before he takes them away!"

CHAPTER 6

A Living Dinosaur!

Back at the cave the next day, Henry found the ladder where he had left it. The children helped one another scramble through the first narrow passage.

"Wait. Let's listen for footsteps," said Henry.

"Or dinosaur steps," said Violet. She smiled nervously.

"Watch will let us know if there's something or someone around," Jessie reminded them. They continued until they arrived at the cavern where they had found the tracks.

"Let's start in here," suggested Henry. "We'll look more carefully this time."

"Watch isn't barking, so I guess nobody is inside," said Jessie. She let Watch lead the way into the cavern while the others closely followed.

Inside the cavern, they looked around for other clues. Violet took photos of the tracks in the mud. Then she noticed a large hole in the wall near the tracks.

"Look, there's a hole here," she said. "And there are more of the strange tracks. They lead into the hole!"

"Good job, Violet," said Jessie. "We missed that yesterday."

"Are we going in there?" asked Benny.

"Let me check first," said Henry. "I'll take Watch with me."

The children waited nervously as Henry ducked inside the hole. After a few seconds, he called to them that everything was okay. The three children crawled inside the hole. The small passage opened up into another room. It led to another passageway.

"Caves are very complicated!" said Benny.

"I'm adding it all to my cave map," said Violet. "It's starting to get confusing!"

"Look, there's a bowl of water," said Jessie. She shined her flashlight on a big white bowl.

"There's a name on the bowl," said Benny. "*Sweet Pea.*"

"I wonder who Sweet Pea is," said Violet.

Just then Watch began to whine. Then a loud booming sound filled the room.

"What is that noise?" asked Jessie. "Why isn't Watch barking?"

A shadow appeared in the passageway and Watch walked inside, wagging his tail. Then he backed out, followed by a strange creature.

"Oh my, what is that?" asked Violet. She ducked behind Jessie.

"I think this is Sweet Pea," whispered Jessie.

All the children huddled together as a strange creature walked toward them. It was a large bird with two long legs and three-toed feet. Long, shaggy gray-brown feathers covered the bird's bulky body and long neck. It had piercing orange-red eyes. The creature looked at each of the children and grunted.

"Is Sweet Pea a real dinosaur?" asked Benny.

The bird approached Benny. She poked at the pockets in his vest. He cringed.

"Sweet Pea is an emu," laughed Henry. "I've read about them in school. They're from Australia."

"What is she doing here?" asked Violet. Sweet Pea turned to stare at her. The bird was taller than Violet. Violet backed up a few steps and Sweet Pea followed, bending over to nudge at Violet's pack.

"Sweet Pea must be Dan's pet," said Jessie. She remembered Dan's funny little smile when Violet asked him about the tracks. "I think he pretended he didn't know anything about the tracks just to tease us."

"I think she likes us," said Benny. "And she really likes Violet." Benny laughed as Sweet Pea kept nudging at Violet's pack. Violet's eyes were wide and she stayed very still.

"H-h-huh-hullo, S-s-s-sweet P-p-p-pea," she stammered as the emu pecked at her pack.

"Ah! I think she wants that corn in your pack," said Jessie. She reached into Violet's pack and retrieved the plastic bag of corn.

She put some in her hand and showed it to Sweet Pea, then tossed the kernels onto the floor. Sweet Pea began to peck at them. She scratched at the cavern floor as she ate.

Violet let out a big breath. "Thank you, Jessie," she said. "Sweet Pea seems friendly, but she is a big bird!"

"I still think Sweet Pea is a dinosaur," said Benny.

"She does look like a dinosaur relative," said Henry. "That must have been her we heard scratching yesterday."

"Was she also the shadow we saw?" asked Jessie.

"I don't know," said Henry. "Look, she's going into that passage. Let's follow her."

Watch led the way as they followed Sweet Pea through the passage and into a smaller cavern.

"Oh no! Another room!" said Violet. She added the room to her cave map. "Look!" Violet pointed at a cloth bag behind some rocks.

The children opened the bag. Inside were pieces of rock with bones embedded in them. They had labels taped on them. Henry read one label out loud. "This one says *51 E.B.*"

"These are the stolen bones!" cried Benny. "Sweet Pea showed us where they are!"

"We found the bones," said Jessie. "Now we have to figure out who stole them and put them here." Jessie looked around the dark room with her headlight. She pointed at an object on the floor. "What's that?"

Violet took a photo of the object. Then she picked it up. "It's a chisel!" she said.

"It looks just like the one we saw in Dinosaur Dan's collection," said Jessie.

"So it must be Dinosaur Dan's chisel and Dinosaur Dan's pet emu," said Henry. "It seems that Dinosaur Dan might be the one who took Elliot's bones."

"He sure was mad at Elliot," said Violet. "Maybe we should go talk to him again."

"We'll leave Elliot's bones here," said Henry.

"We can get them on our way back," agreed Jessie.

"Let's take the chisel to show Dinosaur Dan," said Violet. "We can ask if it belongs to him."

"Good idea, Violet," said Henry. "Okay, let's go!"

"Where do we go?" asked Benny. He looked around. "We've been in so many rooms and passages that I'm lost!"

"We aren't lost," said Violet. She showed Benny the map she had drawn in her sketchbook.

"Oh good!" said Benny. "Let's follow Violet's map."

The children headed back through the passages and rooms to the main passageway.

"Look, Sweet Pea is following us," said Benny. "I bet she would like to have some more of that corn!"

Watch ran ahead as they traveled down the passageway to the big cavern at the end. Dinosaur Dan was busy digging outside.

"I see you kids got caught by my watch-bird this time," he said. Dinosaur Dan laughed as Sweet Pea nuzzled Watch, and Benny petted the big bird on her neck. "And she seems to like you. That's interesting."

"Why is it interesting?" asked Benny.

"Sweet Pea is usually shy," said Dinosaur Dan. "And she can be pretty grumpy. At least that's how she acts around Jolanda."

"Do you mean Jolanda Hogan?" asked Jessie.

"Yeah, Jolanda brings me supplies about once a week or so," said Dinosaur Dan. "She also buys bones from me. Sweet Pea always tries to bite her. I used to distract Sweet Pea with lots of corn when Jolanda came around. Finally I just started leaving her back here when I met Jolanda at the campsite."

"So Jolanda knows that you have a dig?" asked Henry.

"Jolanda knows I have a dig, but she doesn't know where it is. Nobody does. Well, except for you kids." He looked at Sweet Pea. The big bird was nudging at Violet's pack again and grunting. "But I guess that's all right if you can keep my secret."

"Sure we can!" said Benny. "We're good at keeping secrets."

Violet pulled the chisel out of her pack and handed it to Henry.

"We found this chisel in one of the rooms in the cave," said Henry. He handed the chisel to Dinosaur Dan.

"Well, look at that," said Dinosaur Dan. He turned the chisel over in his big hands. "I have a few of these, but this isn't one of mine. See the initials on the handle?" He held the chisel up for the children to see.

"It has a *B* and an *H*," said Benny.

"That's right, young man," said Dinosaur Dan. "That stands for Bones Hogan. He was a famous dinosaur digger around here many years ago. He made his own chisels."

"We went to his museum!" said Benny. "There were a lot of bones in there."

"That's where we met Jolanda Hogan," said Jessie.

"Jolanda's great-granddaddy used to own all the land around here," said Dinosaur Dan. "Sometimes when I dig out here in the heat, chiseling and scraping for hours, I think about old Bones Hogan. He keeps me going. Do you know why?" Dinosaur Dan looked around at the Alden children.

"Why?" Benny was the first to ask.

"Bones Hogan made some of the biggest discoveries ever," said Dinosaur Dan. "If he could do that, even when he was over eighty years old, I figured so could I." He turned the chisel over in his hand. "I wonder what it was doing back in there." He frowned and studied the old tool.

Violet studied Dan's face. She thought he looked like he really was confused.

Dan shrugged. "I'm here to search for bones. Do you kids want to help?"

"You bet we do!" said Benny.

"Well then, follow me," said Dinosaur Dan. He returned the chisel to Violet and trudged ahead. He waved for the children to follow.

"We're right behind you!" called Jessie. She turned to her siblings. "Dinosaur Dan seems to tell the truth, but then he changes the subject."

"Maybe he's the bone thief," Henry pointed to Sweet Pea, who had wandered back to the cave entrance. She ducked inside.

"That's true," said Violet. "But Dinosaur Dan really looked confused about that chisel."

"But right now we can dig for bones!" said Benny. They headed to where Dinosaur Dan was waiting for them.

"Look at this, Benny," said Dinosaur Dan. He held up a jawbone that was surrounded by rock. "This is my big secret. I think this jawbone is part of an undiscovered dinosaur!"

"Wow," said Benny. "Can we help?"

"Yes, you can," said Dinosaur Dan. "I need to move this rock slab. I've got ropes and wood planks already set up. We'll use them for skids. The slab will just slide out of the way."

"What should we do?" asked Henry.

"Just help guide the slab while I drive my ATV," said Dinosaur Dan. "Here we go!"

Dinosaur Dan jumped into his ATV and slowly drove forward. The ropes pulled tight, then the big slab of rock started to move. The children helped to keep the rock on the skids. When the rock was moved and out of the way, everyone looked at what was underneath it.

"As I live and breathe," said Dinosaur Dan. "Will you look at that!"

CHAPTER 7

A New Suspect

They all stared at the nearly complete dinosaur skeleton emerging from the rock. Watch sniffed and scratched at the dirt.

"Hey there, Watch! You be careful!" said Dinosaur Dan. Dan petted Watch on the head. "Kids, I'll bet Bones Hogan is smiling right now. This may be my best find ever."

"And we helped!" said Benny.

"Yes, you did. Thank you very much," said Dinosaur Dan. "I'll get a tent over this old boy and start working on it this afternoon when

I get back from meeting with Mr. Gordon." He chuckled. "I'm going to be chiseling on this thing for a very long time!"

"We're very happy about your find," said Jessie.

"Don't forget our secret," said Dinosaur Dan.

"We won't forget," promised Benny.

"We'll see you again soon," said Henry.

"Sure, you bet," mumbled Dinosaur Dan. He stood staring at the huge skeleton embedded in the rock.

"He's already intent on his new find," whispered Henry as they returned to the cave. "No wonder they call him Dinosaur Dan!"

They headed back to the cavern where the stolen bones were stored. Sweet Pea followed them.

"What do we know about these missing bones so far?" asked Henry. "Do you think that Dan took them and put them here?"

"He said he was going to meet Mr. Gordon today," said Jessie. "If it's to sell these stolen bones, he'll be here soon to get them!"

"Wait," said Violet. "I think that Dinosaur Dan is innocent."

"Why?" asked Jessie. "Dinosaur Dan could have made his way from his end of the cave to the ranch side and stolen the bones. Then he could have stashed them in this cavern."

"I know!" cried Benny. "Dan can't fit through the narrow passage!"

"Oh, that's true," said Henry. "Dan is a tall man."

"Okay," said Jessie. "If Dinosaur Dan isn't the thief, then who is?"

"We'll have to keep looking!" said Henry. "Let's go."

Henry grabbed the bag with Elliot's missing bones and they made their way back to the ranch.

***

"I was just thinking that it's time for lunch," said Elliot when he saw the children approaching the shop. "Oh! Is that my bag?"

"We found your dinosaur bones!" said Benny.

Elliot ran to meet them as Henry set the bag on the ground.

"Wow! Thank you so much!" Elliot exclaimed. "Where did you find it?" He rummaged through the bag and examined the fossils.

"The bag of bones was deep inside the cave," said Jessie.

"Sweet Pea showed us the way!" said Benny.

Elliot looked at Benny curiously. "Who or what is Sweet Pea?" he asked.

"Sweet Pea is Dinosaur Dan's pet emu," said Violet.

"Dinosaur Dan sounds like an interesting fellow," said Elliot. "Well, this is the best news I've ever had. Let's go to the diner to celebrate!"

"Sure!" said Benny.

Grandfather had work to do, so he stayed back at the house with Watch, while the children rode with Elliot to Hogan's Museum and Diner. As the jeep drove along, Jessie thought about finding the bag of bones. If Dan wasn't the thief, who was?

At the diner they sat down and looked at their menus. A young man introduced himself as Mickey.

"Let's have pizza!" said Benny. "Half

pepperoni and half vege…vege…"

"Vegetarian," said Violet. She smiled at her little brother.

Mickey took their order and a few minutes later brought the pizza.

"Oh, look," said Jessie. "Isn't that Mr. Gordon?"

Elliot turned to look as the buyer headed toward the museum door. "Yes, it is," he said. "Let's go and say hello when we're finished eating."

When Elliot and the children entered the museum, they saw Jolanda sorting through a blue crate. Mr. Gordon was talking to her. When she looked up and saw the children approaching, she quickly stashed the crate behind the counter. Mr. Gordon turned and smiled.

"Hello there, Elliot," he said. "I see you still have visitors."

"Yes, we were just having lunch," said Elliot. He smiled at Jolanda, but she looked away. "I'm glad to find you here," Elliot continued. "I still want to tell you about that recent find."

"Yes, Elliot, of course, let's sit down and

discuss your find," said Warren. "I can't wait to hear all about it!"

Elliot and Warren headed back to the diner to talk.

"It's nice to see you again," said Jolanda to the Aldens. She reached under the counter and brought out a handful of small items. "You might like these trilobite fossils for your collection," she said, spreading the little fossils out on the counter.

"Trilobites are sea creatures," said Henry. He handed one to Benny. "We should get one for your fossil collection, Benny!"

"It looks like a monster centipede," said Benny. "I like this trilobite!"

"Great! Let's go ring up your purchase at the diner," said Jolanda.

Henry and Benny followed Jolanda. Violet and Jessie stayed behind. They both peeked behind the counter and spotted the blue crate.

"That crate looks like the crates we saw in Dinosaur Dan's collection," said Jessie.

"Yes, it does," said Violet. "And look, there's something written on the side."

"*Bambi*," said Jessie. "How funny."

"I wonder why Jolanda hid the crate when she saw us?" asked Violet. "Mr. Gordon probably got the crate from Dinosaur Dan at their meeting today."

Violet pulled out her camera and took a photo of the crate. Then she looked at the wall behind the counter.

"Look," she said. Violet pointed to a photo of a group of people. There was a red arrow on the photo that pointed to a young woman. Someone had written: *Me graduating!*

"That must be Jolanda when she graduated from college," said Jessie, studying the photo. "This man in the back row looks familiar too." She pointed to a red-haired man smiling at the camera. "I can't figure out who he is though."

"Hey kids, time to head back," said Elliot from behind where they stood. He was excited. "Mr. Gordon is coming to the ranch later. I need to get back to my shop right away!"

"Then let's go!" said Jessie.

***

"Maybe we can help you get ready to meet with Mr. Gordon," Jessie offered.

Elliot pulled the jeep into the driveway of the ranch. "Sure, you can help me get things ready," he said. "That would be very helpful. Thanks to you four, I now have almost a complete dinosaur to show him!" He smiled.

The children helped Elliot arrange the bones.

Benny proudly added the toe bone that he had found. "Now it looks like a whole dinosaur!" he said.

"Well, there are a few parts still missing," said Elliot. "I hope to find more. We'll see what Mr. Gordon says about what I have so far."

"Here he comes," said Henry.

A truck pulled up next to the shop and Mr. Gordon got out. The children greeted him and then walked back to the house.

"I wonder what Mr. Gordon and Jolanda were talking about," said Jessie. "And why she hid the blue crate when she saw us."

"If Mr. Gordon bought whatever is in the blue crate from Dinosaur Dan, there would be nothing to hide," said Henry. "It seems that Mr. Gordon might be up to something."

"Jolanda seems like she is up to something too," said Jessie.

"She doesn't seem to like Elliot very much," said Violet.

"Oh!" said Jessie.

"What is it?" asked Violet.

"I think I know who that man was in the graduation photo, the one who looked familiar," said Jessie. "It's Elliot!"

"So, Jolanda was in Elliot's graduating class," said Henry. "That is very interesting."

"Everything about Jolanda is interesting," said Jessie.

"Let's go back and visit Dinosaur Dan," suggested Violet. "Maybe he can tell us more about Jolanda Hogan and Mr. Gordon."

CHAPTER 8

Big Discovery

Dinosaur Dan was outside when the children returned to his side of the cave. He was happily chipping away at the newly found dinosaur.

"I'm so glad you came back!" he said when he saw the Aldens.

"How is your excavation coming along?" asked Henry.

"Very well, thank you, Henry," said Dinosaur Dan. "And I have some very exciting news about this dinosaur!"

"Oh, what is the news?" asked Benny.

"This dinosaur is an ornithomimid like none ever found before," said Dinosaur Dan. "I checked all my books and journals."

"They're called ornithomimids because they remind us of ostriches and emus," said Henry. "People call them bird mimics."

"That's right," said Dinosaur Dan. "Maybe this dinosaur is Sweet Pea's ancestor!" He laughed. "Come on, kids. You can help me chip around this bone I'm working on. I'll show you how it's done."

The children followed Dinosaur Dan's directions. They carefully picked at the delicate bones.

"How was your meeting with Mr. Gordon?" asked Henry.

"Oh, it was okay. He didn't buy anything though," said Dinosaur Dan. "To tell you the truth, I don't trust him."

"Why not?" asked Jessie.

"Oh, he's just nosy, that's all," said Dinosaur Dan. "I met him at the old Hogan Museum last year. He asked too many questions about where I was working."

"How about Jolanda?" asked Jessie. "Do you trust her?"

"Jolanda's all right, I guess," said Dinosaur Dan. "Not that Sweet Pea agrees with me!" He chuckled. Sweet Pea was pecking at the grass nearby. She looked up and grunted.

Just then Dinosaur Dan's cell phone rang. He fumbled around in his overalls and pulled out the phone.

"Hello?" he said. "Oh, hey there, Jolanda. Say, I missed you yesterday but I was glad you could send somebody in your place. I was out of food for Sweet Pea!"

The children worked and tried not to listen to the call. But it was hard not to hear what Dinosaur Dan was saying to Jolanda.

"Okay, then I'll see you next week. I might have something exciting to show you. Good-bye." Dinosaur Dan chuckled. "That was Jolanda. It's funny that we were just talking about her." He looked around. "Now maybe you strong young people can help me move these crates back to my cave."

The children helped carry blue crates back to the cave. Dan and Henry carried the biggest one. They set the crates down and Dan looked around. He scratched his head.

"Hey! Where are my bambiraptor bones?" he said. "They were in a crate right over there. I've been robbed!"

"Was the crate also blue and marked *Bambi*?" asked Violet.

"Yes, it was," said Dinosaur Dan. "And I know who stole them!"

"Who?" asked Henry.

"Elliot Boyce. Who else?" cried Dinosaur Dan. "You said he just moved in nearby. He's trying to frame me as a thief. He's probably the one who upset Sweet Pea."

"What do you mean?" asked Violet.

"When I got back from meeting Jolanda's helper last evening, Sweet Pea was pacing around the cave," said Dinosaur Dan. "She kept pecking at the ground and grunting. It was not her nice grunt, mind you. Sweet Pea has a grumpy grunt too."

"She must have seen the thief," said Henry.

"You mean she must have seen Elliot Boyce!" said Dinosaur Dan. "But, say, how did you kids know that the crate was labeled

Bambi?" Dinosaur Dan looked at the Aldens. He was frowning again.

"It's a long story," said Jessie, "but we saw Mr. Gordon with that crate earlier today."

Violet pulled out her camera and showed Dinosaur Dan the photo she had taken. He shook his head.

"That's my crate and those are my bones," he said. "What was Mr. Gordon doing with them? I bet he got them from that thief, Elliot!"

"We'll get your bambiraptor bones for you," said Henry. "Please don't worry."

"Well, if you can, I'd be grateful," said Dinosaur Dan. "I can't leave my site with a thieving neighbor nosing around." Sweet Pea walked over and nuzzled Dinosaur Dan.

The children headed back through the cave.

"I know the way by heart now," said Benny.

"We still need to be very careful," warned Jessie. "Let's stick together as always."

"Dinosaur Dan was sure Elliot stole his bambiraptor bones," said Henry. "But I don't see how."

"We saw Mr. Gordon with the crate,"

said Violet. "Maybe we can ask him where he got it."

"Mr. Gordon could be the one who stole Elliot's bones *and* Dan's bones," said Jessie.

"Why did Jolanda hide the blue crate when we appeared?" asked Henry. "Did she know stolen bones were inside?"

"I just thought of something," said Violet. "We heard Dinosaur Dan tell Jolanda he was sorry to miss her yesterday."

"Dinosaur Dan left Sweet Pea behind. She was grumpy when he got back," said Benny. "Sweet Pea doesn't like Jolanda!"

"Maybe that was Jolanda in the cave entrance yesterday," said Jessie.

"And she saw us and had to hide!" said Benny.

"It looks like Mr. Gordon and Jolanda are working together," said Henry. "Let's go tell Elliot about another dinosaur bone theft."

"That's a good plan," said Jessie. "And maybe it's time for Elliot and Dinosaur Dan to meet face to face."

CHAPTER 9

Old Friends

"There you are," said Grandfather when he saw the children approaching the sunny deck. "Elliot and I made hotdogs and beans for an early supper. We thought we were going to have it all to ourselves."

"Oh no! We love hotdogs and beans!" said Benny.

Grandfather chuckled as they headed inside to eat. While they ate, Elliot told them that Mr. Gordon had been very interested in his find.

"He took photos of everything," said Elliot. "He said that he would be in touch."

"That's very exciting," said Grandfather. "I know you work hard to make a living as a paleontologist."

"I think we should celebrate," said Benny. "Let's get ice cream for dessert."

"Benny, that's a good idea," said Elliot. "There's a little ice cream parlor in town. Let's go!"

"Watch and I will stay here," said Grandfather. "Have fun!"

"We'll bring you a milkshake," promised Benny.

"Make that chocolate, please," said Grandfather, smiling.

On the way to town, Henry asked Elliot if he ever wondered what happened to his friend Dan.

"I don't know, and I don't care," said Elliot. "Why do you ask?"

"Your neighbor Dinosaur Dan is your old classmate," said Jessie.

"Ha!" said Elliot. "I guess we know who stole my dinosaur bones now! Dan is still trying to ruin my life."

"There's more to the story," said Henry.

When they got to the ice cream parlor, the children explained that Dinosaur Dan was too large to fit through the small passageway and steal Elliot's bones.

"Someone stole some of Dinosaur Dan's bones too," said Jessie. "When we told him you live next door, he figured it was you."

"You must be joking! He called me a thief after what he did in college?" said Elliot.

"He says you tried to take all the credit for your project," said Henry. "That's why he left."

"Huh?" asked Elliot. "I did no such thing!"

"We also found a small chisel next to your stolen bones," said Jessie. "It's marked *B.H.* for Bones Hogan."

"You're kidding!" said Elliot. "I have one of the old handmade Bones Hogan chisels. I treasure it."

"Have you noticed that it was missing?" asked Violet.

"Nope. It stays in a showcase in my house," said Elliot. "And that case is always locked."

"Dinosaur Dan said that it wasn't his either," said Henry. "I wonder where that chisel came from."

"So you kids think that Dinosaur Dan couldn't get to my side of the cave," said Elliot. He finished his ice cream cone with a gulp. "But I'd like to chat with him anyway. I think my old friend and I have some catching up to do."

Jessie looked at Violet and nodded. Violet took out her notepad where she had written Dinosaur Dan's phone number. She asked to borrow Elliot's cell phone and dialed the number.

"Hello, Dinosaur Dan!" she said. "It's me, Violet. May we see you at your campsite? We have someone for you to meet." She waited a few seconds. "Okay, we're on our way!" Violet hung up and looked at everyone. "He'll be there waiting."

"I guess we better head over there now," said Jessie.

"Don't forget the milkshake for Grandfather!" said Benny. "Chocolate! And a bag of ice to put it in so it doesn't melt on the way!"

They ordered the milkshake and headed back to the jeep.

Elliot drove them past his ranch. Henry noticed a truck pass by in the other lane. It looked familiar. Then Elliot turned into the next road. It was a dusty gravel drive that had obviously been used recently.

They bumped along until they arrived at a campsite. Dinosaur Dan and Sweet Pea were waiting.

"They call you Dinosaur Dan now, huh?" Elliot said.

"Well, look who it is, a few years older but just as tiresome," said Dinosaur Dan.

Sweet Pea spotted Violet and started nuzzling her. "I don't have the bag of corn with me," Violet whispered. She petted the big bird on the neck.

"Tiresome? How do you expect me to be? You almost cost me my college degree!" said Elliot.

"What are you squawking about?" asked Dinosaur Dan. "You took my name off our research project. You made it look like you did all the work yourself."

"I did what?" asked Elliot. The children noticed that he looked very surprised. "You abandoned me and took all your notes!" said Elliot. "I had to do it alone."

Dinosaur Dan scratched his head. "Well, I sure didn't take my name off of anything," he said.

"Well, if you didn't, who did?" asked Elliot.

"Good question," said Dinosaur Dan. Just

then, a truck pulled in next to Elliot's jeep. "Look, we have company."

Mr. Gordon got out and walked over to the group. Henry realized that it was the truck he had seen earlier.

"Hey, I sort of followed you folks," said Mr. Gordon. "I saw you turn onto this road and decided to come back and see what you were up to."

"See?" said Dinosaur Dan, looking at the Aldens. "The guy is nosy. Like I said."

"My business is seeing what you diggers are up to," said Mr. Gordon. He smiled. "So what did I miss?"

"We were just getting reacquainted," said Elliot.

"We're old friends," said Dinosaur Dan. He patted Elliot on the back.

"We have a question for you if that's okay," said Henry.

"Please ask," said Mr. Gordon.

"We saw you looking through a crate of bones at the museum today," said Henry.

"And when Jolanda saw us, she quickly put the crate under the counter," said Jessie.

"Oh yes!" said Mr. Gordon. "I thought it was odd, but Jolanda said the bones were a secret. I didn't want to ruin my chance to buy them."

"What kind of bones were they?" asked Dinosaur Dan. "Were they perhaps bambiraptor bones?"

"Why yes, they were!" said Mr. Gordon. "I'd like to purchase them."

"They were stolen from me," said Dinosaur Dan. "You're saying that you aren't the one who stole them?"

"No, no, no!" said Mr. Gordon. "I didn't steal anything."

Just then Sweet Pea clumped over to Mr. Gordon and nuzzled his pocket.

"Oh, hello there," he said. He stroked Sweet Pea as she nibbled at his jacket. "I'll bet you want the corn in my pocket." He pulled out a handful of corn and tossed it on the ground. Sweet Pea gobbled it up.

"Where did you get that corn?" asked Dinosaur Dan. "That's the special food that I buy for Sweet Pea!"

"Jolanda had a bowl of it behind the

counter at the museum. I grabbed a handful, thinking it was snack food of some kind," said Mr. Gordon. "It's a little rough on the teeth, I must say." He chuckled.

"Jolanda brings it to me in big bags," said Dinosaur Dan. "Why would she have a bowl of it?"

"I don't know," said Mr. Gordon. "She didn't see me take it."

"Like I said, nosy," grumbled Dinosaur Dan.

Mr. Gordon smiled. "I'm a snoop, that's for sure," he admitted.

Jessie turned to Elliot and Dinosaur Dan. "Do either of you remember Jolanda from college?" she asked.

"No," said Elliot. "Was she there?"

"Yes," said Violet. "There's a photo in the museum of your graduating class. Jolanda is there, and so are you, Elliot."

"I left before that photo was taken," said Dinosaur Dan. "But I don't remember Jolanda either. I guess people change when they get older." He laughed. "Not me, I was already an old guy!"

"Jolanda must look different now," said

Elliot. "I don't remember her at all."

"Maybe you never noticed her," said Violet.

"It was a big school," said Elliot. "There were a lot of paleontology students."

"But we think that maybe Jolanda remembers you," said Henry.

"Let's go see Jolanda in the morning," said Jessie. "It looks as if she has something to do with everything that has happened to you both."

CHAPTER 10

The Clues Add Up

The next morning after breakfast Henry, Jessie, Violet, Benny, and Elliot piled into the jeep. Watch jumped in with them.

"Watch wants to come with us this time," said Jessie.

"Grandfather said he wanted to go bird watching today," said Violet. "I think he's enjoying the peace and quiet."

They picked up Dinosaur Dan at his campsite. On the way to the museum, Elliot mentioned that it would be fun to see his old

friend's dig.

"Oh, you bet, Elliot," said Dinosaur Dan. "I'd be happy to show it to you. And we can get caught up on all those lost years."

The children smiled. They were happy that the two men were friends again.

Jolanda was unlocking the door to the museum when they arrived. She headed inside and closed the door.

"Did she see us? asked Violet.

"I'm not sure," said Jessie. "If she did, that was not very nice to ignore us."

They found that the door was unlocked and headed into the museum.

"Hello. Are you open?" asked Elliot.

Jolanda popped up from behind the counter. "Oh," she said. She shoved something behind her with her feet. "Can I do something for you people?"

"We wanted to ask you a few questions, Jolanda," said Dinosaur Dan.

"Is that so?" asked Jolanda.

"We went to the same college," said Elliot. He pointed at the class photo hanging on the wall. "That's me in the photo."

"I remember you," said Jolanda. "Not that you paid any attention to me, Elliot Boyce. You and Dan spent all your time trespassing on my great-grandfather's land. Those bones you were digging up and claiming as your own were part of the Hogan legacy!"

"The land was leased by the college," said Dinosaur Dan. "Your great-granddaddy deeded it to them years ago. We had every right to dig there."

"Not as far as I was concerned," said Jolanda. "That coelurosaur you two found was on our family's original land. Credit belonged to the Hogans, not you."

"That really made you mad, didn't it?" asked Henry.

Jolanda glared at Henry. "You bet it did, kiddo. And I got even."

"You did something to our presentation?" asked Elliot. "Did you take Dan's name off the project somehow?"

Jolanda laughed. "It took you long enough to figure that out," she said. "One day I saw you leave the library without logging out of the computer there. I found your files and removed Dan's name from your presentation."

"Why would you do such a thing?" asked Dinosaur Dan. "I left college because of your nasty prank!"

"Like I said, you men are nothing but thieves," said Jolanda. "Maybe you need to leave my museum." She walked over to the door. "All of you, please leave."

Henry quickly ducked behind the counter. He grabbed the blue crate and plunked it onto the counter. "First I think we need to talk about this," he said.

"Those are my bambiraptor bones!" cried Dan. "Why did you steal them from me, Jolanda?"

"Prove they're yours," said Jolanda. "I dare you."

Violet took out her camera and showed the photo she took of the crates in Dan's cave. The crate marked *Bambi* was in view. "The crate was in Dan's cave yesterday," said Violet. "You sneaked in later and stole it."

Jolanda glared at Violet. "You can't prove that I took them," she said.

"You knew where Dan's site was because your great-grandfather used to own this land," said Henry.

Jolanda shook her head. "I have no idea what you're talking about," she said.

Violet pulled out the bag of corn. "And you kept Sweet Pea from biting you by feeding her corn that you took from Dan's supply," she said.

Jolanda rolled her eyes. "You kids sure know how to make up a story," she said.

"We found an old chisel in the cave," said Violet.

"The chisel was marked *B.H.*," said Henry.

Jessie pointed at a display of chisels hanging on the wall. "It looks like it used to hang in that empty space on the wall, next to the others just like it."

Jolanda's eyes got wide. "That chisel is my property. You better give it back!" she cried.

"We found it right next to the crate of bones stolen from Elliot," said Jessie.

Jolanda shook her fist. "I must have dropped it. I always have it with me. It brings me good luck."

"Why would you steal our dinosaur bones, Jolanda?" asked Elliot.

"Let me tell you something," said Jolanda, shaking. "My great-grandfather's legacy must never be forgotten. I was willing to do whatever it took to make sure that didn't happen!"

"I don't think that Bones Hogan would be happy that you stole things," said Violet.

"And nearly cost me my college degree," said Elliot.

"And caused me to leave college!" said Dinosaur Dan.

Jolanda looked stunned. She didn't say anything for a moment, like she was thinking hard. Then she took a deep breath and sighed. She lowered her head sadly. "I'm sorry about that," she said. "Violet, you're right. Bones wouldn't be happy with me at all." She looked around the room. "It's just that my great-grandfather's legacy is slowly disappearing. I want to honor him by writing a book, but this museum and diner bog me down. Then it seemed like you were coming in to take whatever you wanted..."

"That was no reason to steal from us and cause trouble between friends," said Elliot.

"I know that now," said Jolanda quietly. "I'm very sorry."

"Jolanda, you know me. If you needed help, you could have asked," said Dan.

"Help?" Jolanda looked at Dan curiously. "How could you to help me?"

"I've made a pretty penny peddling my dinosaur finds," said Dinosaur Dan. "Maybe I could invest in your museum and diner and get you some help."

"Oh!" said Jolanda. "You would do that?"

"Sure," said Dinosaur Dan. "And Elliot might be interested in being the museum curator. How about it, Elliot?"

"That would be great!" said Elliot. "I'd be honored to run the museum and tell visitors about Bones Hogan."

"Yes!" said Jolanda. "You could work on your finds in the shop out back. "Everything you need is there." She smiled at Elliot.

Elliot smiled shyly back at Jolanda.

"Maybe we had some differences, Jolanda," said Dan. "But there is one thing we agree on, and that's honoring your great-granddaddy's legacy."

"That would be wonderful," said Jolanda. "I can turn the place over to you two, Mickey can hire extra help, and I can write my book!"

"Then I reckon it's settled," said Dan. He put out his hand and Jolanda shook it.

"I'll give back your bambiraptor bones, of course," said Jolanda. "I'm very embarrassed about all the trouble I caused you two. And now you're being so nice to me."

"Sometimes good things just start off on the wrong foot," said Dan.

"You're right about that!" said Elliot.

Benny smiled at everyone. "Is it time for lunch yet?" he asked.

Everyone joined in the laughter. "Yes, Benny," said Jolanda. "I can make you some sandwiches."

"Thank you," said Jessie.

"We'll help you!" said Violet.

"We can take them back to Dinosaur Dan's dig site," said Benny. "That will be fun!"

Everyone headed into the diner and helped Jolanda prepare a picnic lunch.

"We'll work out the details tomorrow," said Dinosaur Dan. "How does that sound?"

"Okay," said Jolanda. "I'm excited to get started on my book, but I can wait one more day!" She smiled and shook Dan's hand again.

Elliot turned to the children and grinned. "We sure are grateful to you kids for figuring out what was going on!"

"We like to solve mysteries," said Violet.

"Especially a mystery about dinosaurs," said Benny.

***

Elliot stopped by the ranch to pick up Grandfather on the way to Dinosaur Dan's site. Along the way he and Elliot talked about the Hogan Museum and Diner.

"I think you and I should do more than just invest in the museum. I think we should buy that place," said Dan. "We can be partners. What do you say?"

"I think that's a great idea," said Elliot. "The one good thing Jolanda did was try to keep the memory of Bones Hogan alive. She just didn't go about it the right way."

The friends shook hands as they entered the dinosaur valley.

"Wow," said Elliot. He looked around and gasped. "This valley is like a dinosaur museum!"

"It's an amazing place," said Dinosaur Dan. "And wait until you see what the kids and I uncovered."

Dan led them to the ornithomimid remains and smiled. Elliot examined it and agreed that it was not like anything that had ever been found before.

"So what are you going to name it?" asked Grandfather. "Whoever finds a new dinosaur gets to give it a name."

Benny raised his hand, grinning.

"Do you have a suggestion for a name, Benny?" asked Dinosaur Dan.

"Yes," said Benny. "I think we should call it a Bennysaurus!"

THE BOXCAR CHILDREN®
Fan Club

Join the Boxcar Fan Club!

Visit **boxcarchildren.com** and receive a free goodie
bag when you sign up. You'll receive occasional
newsletters and be eligible to win prizes
and more! Sign up today!

Don't Forget!

The Boxcar Children audiobooks are also available!
Find them at your local bookstore, or visit
oasisaudio.com for more information.

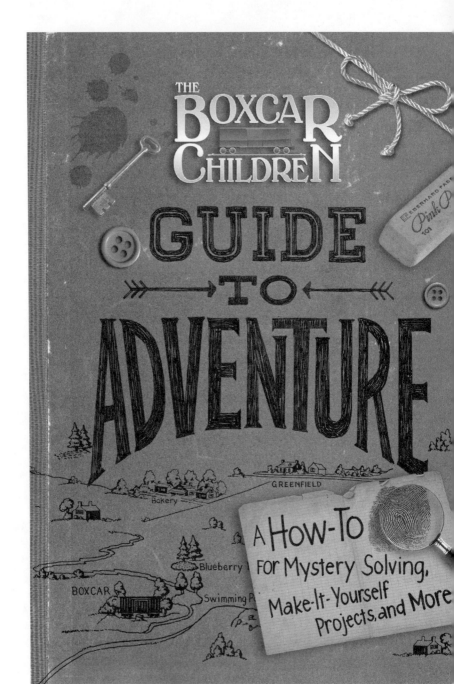

THE **BOXCAR CHILDREN**

GUIDE ⟫⟶TO⟵⟪ ADVENTURE

A How-To For Mystery Solving, Make-It-Yourself Projects, and More

ISBN: 9780807509050, $12.

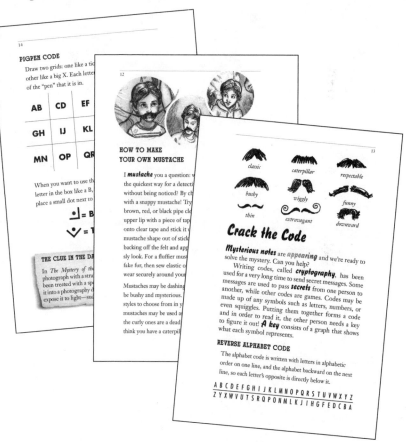

Discover how the Boxcar Children's adventures began!

THE **BOXCAR CHILDREN** BEGINNING

"Fans will enjoy this picture of life 'before.'"
—*Publishers Weekly*

Before they were the Boxcar Children, Henry, Jessie, Violet, and Benny Alden lived with their parents on Fair Meadow Farm.

NEWBERY MEDAL-WINNER
PATRICIA MACLACHLAN

PB ISBN: 9780807566176, $5.99

The adventures continue in the newest mysteries!

THE

BOXCAR
CHILDREN

THE MYSTERY OF THE WILD WEST BANDIT

Created by
GERTRUDE CHANDLER WARNER

PB ISBN: 9780807587263, $5.99

THE
BOXCAR
CHILDREN

THE MYSTERY OF THE GRINNING GARGOYLE

Created by
GERTRUDE CHANDLER WARNER

PB ISBN: 9780807508930, $5.99

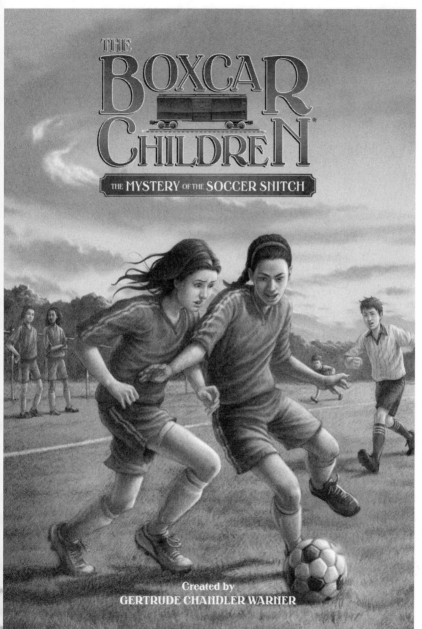

THE BOXCAR CHILDREN

THE MYSTERY OF THE SOCCER SNITCH

Created by
GERTRUDE CHANDLER WARNER

PB ISBN: 9780807508961, $5.99

**Read on for an exclusive sneak peek of the
newest Boxcar Children Mystery!**

A Pop Star Arrives

Be the next big pop star! Audition for Pop Star Sensation *today!* read the giant sign hanging over the entrance to Silver City Mall.

"Are you ready to sing, Violet?" asked twelve-year-old Jessie Alden.

Violet Alden, dressed in her best purple skirt, blushed and hid behind the oldest Alden child, fourteen-year-old Henry. "You're making me nervous," she said shyly.

"Go, Violet!" cheered her younger brother, Benny, who was six. "You can do it!"

Violet's favorite TV show, *Pop Star Sensation*, was holding tryouts in Silver City that day. The show's judges were looking for talented singers who might become the next big music star. Contestants had to be at least Henry's age to compete, so Violet was too young, but she was hoping for the chance to sing on the show, even if it would only be for fun.

Violet and her three siblings were going behind the scenes of *Pop Star Sensation* for the day. Their grandfather had an old friend who was the producer of the show, and he had invited the children to watch the filming. All four of the children were excited, especially Violet, who never missed an episode and sang along to every song.

At ten, Violet was the youngest Alden sister and the shyest of the four children. Although she was bashful—especially in situations like this—Violet was a very talented musician. She played violin, and her ear for music helped her sing very well. Even if Violet was quiet around other people, her siblings had listened to her sing for years.

"Violet," said Benny, "you're the best singer I know. You shouldn't be nervous at all!"

"That's right, Violet," said Jessie. "You're going to do really well. And we'll be here for you."

The Alden children had always supported each other. When they had become orphans, they ran away and lived in an abandoned boxcar in the woods. They had been afraid to live with their grandfather, worrying that he would be a mean man. But when the children realized what a nice man Grandfather Alden was, they were happy to live with him in his big house. He was so nice, in fact, that he had the children's boxcar moved to the backyard for a playhouse.

"And if Grandfather finishes with his business in time," said Henry, "he'll be cheering for you too."

Grandfather had dropped them off at the mall earlier that morning. He had a business meeting to attend elsewhere in Silver City, but he planned to meet up with his grandchildren later that day.

The four Alden children turned and looked behind them. The mall's vast parking lot was filling up with thousands of other people. They had all dressed up to stand out, hoping to look funny or fancy or flashy so that they would get a chance to appear on the TV show. Near the Aldens was a woman with heavy makeup and a hot-pink feather boa wrapped around her neck. Behind her stood a man in a cowboy hat, cowboy boots, and leather cowboy chaps. He twirled a lasso while singing a country-western tune. Behind the cowboy was a family with more children than the Aldens.

"Look, guys," said Benny, pointing at the children, who were all dressed in matching gray outfits and green neckties. "There are seven brothers and sisters in that family!"

"It's not polite to point, Benny," said Jessie. But Jessie was very impressed by the beautiful voices she heard as the family of five sisters and two brothers practiced singing together. The Aldens listened until they became aware of another sound.

From the back of the crowd, a murmur had begun to grow louder. Soon the murmur became a roar of cheers. The Aldens turned to see what all the fuss was about. The crowd moved out of the way for a line of big black cars driving through the mall parking lot.

The cars had black-tinted windows so no one could see inside. The cars made their way to the front entrance, coming to a stop near where the Aldens stood.

"I wonder who's inside," Jessie said.

"I bet it's someone important," said Henry.

"Do you think it might be Madlynn Rose?" Violet asked, naming her favorite singer.

The answer to Violet's question came soon enough. The door to the first black car opened. As soon as the person inside climbed out, the crowd began to boo.

"Why is everyone booing?" Benny asked. "That's not very nice." Neither he nor his siblings booed since all four of them tried to be nice to everyone.

"It's Wilfred Mayflower," said Jessie. "He's *not* very nice."

Wilfred Mayflower was the head judge of *Pop Star Sensation*. He was a short, round man, and to the Alden children, he seemed even shorter and rounder in person. He wore

a spotless white suit and shining white shoes. He also had a very shiny bald head.

Wilfred Mayflower spent each episode of *Pop Star Sensation* hurting contestants' feelings. When many of the contestants finished singing a song, Wilfred would yell, "That was *horrible!*" He had a thick British accent that the Aldens thought made him sound smart and scary at the same time. Violet hoped Wilfred Mayflower would be nice if she ever got the chance to sing for him.

The crowd kept booing Wilfred Mayflower, but he didn't seem to mind. In fact, he seemed to enjoy it. He smiled as the boos grew louder and he waved to the mob of people who booed him. Wilfred reached the entrance to the Silver City Mall just as the door to the next black SUV opened.

GERTRUDE CHANDLER WARNER discovered when she was teaching that many readers who like an exciting story could find no books that were both easy and fun to read. She decided to try to meet this need, and her first book, *The Boxcar Children*, quickly proved she had succeeded.

Miss Warner drew on her own experiences to write the mystery. As a child she spent hours watching trains go by on the tracks opposite her family home. She often dreamed about what it would be like to set up housekeeping in a caboose or freight car—the situation the Alden children find themselves in.

While the mystery element is central to each of Miss Warner's books, she never thought of them as strictly juvenile mysteries. She liked to stress the Aldens' independence and resourcefulness and their solid New England devotion to using up and making do. The Aldens go about most of their adventures with as little adult supervision as possible—something else that delights young readers.

Miss Warner lived in Putnam, Connecticut, until her death in 1979. During her lifetime, she received hundreds of letters from girls and boys telling her how much they liked her books.